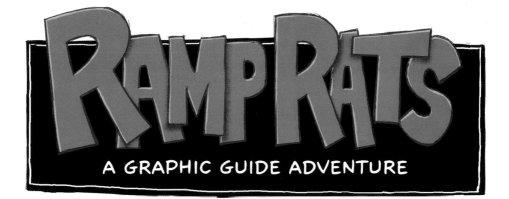

A GRAPHIC GUIDE ADVENTURE

WRITTEN BY
LIAM O'DONNELL

ILLUSTRATED BY
MIKE DEAS

ORCA BOOK PUBLISHERS

For Melanie, a master at Tony Hawk's Pro Skater and so much more. —LOD

Thanks to Jean-Luc Giroux for sharing his knowledge and trying to teach me a 50/50 grind. —MD

ACKNOWLEDGMENTS

Thanks to Marie Campbell for making these adventures a reality.

**Library and Archives Canada Cataloguing in Publication**

O'Donnell, Liam, 1970-
Ramp rats : a graphic guide adventure / written by Liam O'Donnell ;
illustrated by Mike Deas.

ISBN 978-1-55143-880-1 (pbk.).—ISBN 978-1-55469-076-3 (bound)

I. Deas, Michael, 1982- II. Title.

PN6733.O36R34 2008     j741.5'971     C2008-903028-1

First published in the United States, 2008

**Library of Congress Control Number**: 2008934298

**Summary**: Marcus spends the summer teaching his young cousin
to skateboard while bringing the local outlaw bikers to justice.

**Disclaimer:** This book is a work of fiction and is intended for entertainment purposes only. The author and/or publisher accepts no responsibility for misuse or misinterpretation of the information in this book.

Orca Book Publishers gratefully acknowledges the support for its publishing programs provided by the following agencies: the Government of Canada through the Book Publishing Industry Development Program and the Canada Council for the Arts, and the Province of British Columbia through the BC Arts Council and the Book Publishing Tax Credit.

Cover and interior artwork by Mike Deas
Cover layout by Teresa Bubela
Author photo by Melanie McBride • Illustrator photo by Ellen Ho

ORCA BOOK PUBLISHERS
PO Box 5626, STN. B
VICTORIA, BC CANADA
V8R 6S4

ORCA BOOK PUBLISHERS
PO Box 468
CUSTER, WA USA
98240-0468

www.orcabook.com
Printed and bound in China.
11  10  09  08  •  4  3  2  1

3 0088 00011 6854

WE HAVE TO DO SOMETHING ABOUT CRUNCH OR WE WON'T HAVE ANYWHERE TO SKATE THIS SUMMER. OUTSIDE THE SKATE PARK, THIS WHOLE TOWN IS A GIANT NO-SKATE ZONE.

PEMA HAD JUST MOVED TO HILLSIDE LAST YEAR, BUT SHE WAS RIGHT. FOR THE COPS, BUSTING SKATERS WAS A BIGGER SPORT THAN HOCKEY. WITH CRUNCH GUARDING THE PARK, PEMA AND I WERE MORE VULNERABLE THAN A ROOKIE IN OPEN ICE.

THERE'S NOTHING I CAN DO ABOUT CRUNCH. I'VE BEEN HIS FAVORITE PUNCHING BAG SINCE KINDERGARTEN.

YOU COULD TELL YOUR DAD ABOUT IT.

I HAVE! HE JUST TELLS ME TO BE A MAN AND STAND UP TO CRUNCH. EASY FOR HIM TO SAY. HE'S NEVER HAD TO FACE A BULLY AS MEAN AS CRUNCH.

HE HAS A POINT. YOU'VE GOT TO STAND UP TO CRUNCH SOMETIME. NO ONE ELSE CAN DO IT FOR YOU.

LAST TIME I TRIED THAT, CRUNCH REARRANGED MY FACE AND THREW MY SKATEBOARD IN THE LAKE.

CRUNCH ISN'T GOING TO LEAVE YOU ALONE. BESIDES, NEXT TIME YOU WON'T HAVE TO STAND UP TO HIM ALONE. I'LL BE THERE TOO.

YOU CAN PICK UP THE PIECES WHEN CRUNCH IS FINISHED WITH ME!

EVERY TIME CRUNCH BOOTED US FROM THE SKATE PARK, WE ENDED UP BACK AT THE SAME PLACE: SKATING IN FRONT OF MY DAD'S USED TRUCK LOT.

YOU SURE YOUR DAD DOESN'T MIND US SKATING HERE?

WHY WOULD HE MIND?

HANK'S PICKUP PALACE

WATCH IT, KID!

BENNY, GET OFF THE ROAD!!

THAT'S WHY.

WHAT HAVE I TOLD YOU, SON? USE THAT BOARD IN THE SKATE PARK OR I'LL USE IT FOR FIREWOOD. GO GET CLEANED UP. YOUR MOM WILL BE BACK SOON.

ASHLEY AIN'T MY MOM.

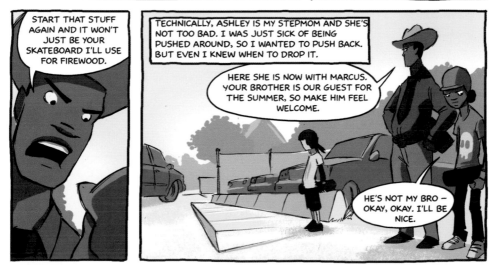

START THAT STUFF AGAIN AND IT WON'T JUST BE YOUR SKATEBOARD I'LL USE FOR FIREWOOD.

TECHNICALLY, ASHLEY IS MY STEPMOM AND SHE'S NOT TOO BAD. I WAS JUST SICK OF BEING PUSHED AROUND, SO I WANTED TO PUSH BACK. BUT EVEN I KNEW WHEN TO DROP IT.

HERE SHE IS NOW WITH MARCUS. YOUR BROTHER IS OUR GUEST FOR THE SUMMER, SO MAKE HIM FEEL WELCOME.

HE'S NOT MY BRO — OKAY, OKAY. I'LL BE NICE.

THAT ALLEY BESIDE MY HOUSE HAD THE STEEPEST HILL IN TOWN. I LOVE RIDING MY BIKE DOWN IT, BUT I'D NEVER TRIED IT ON MY BOARD. I HAD NO IDEA IF I WOULD MAKE IT. GUESS I WAS ABOUT TO FIND OUT.

YAAAHH!

TOC!

AHHHH!

CRASH!

NOW YOU SEE WHY THEY CALL HIM BOUNCE.

AND HE TAUGHT US ANOTHER IMPORTANT LESSON IN SKATING: HOW TO CRASH!

FIRST YOU NEED TO POP A BIG OLLIE. YOU KNOW HOW TO OLLIE, DON'T YOU?

OF COURSE I CAN OLLIE. HERE, I'LL SHOW YOU.

THE OLLIE IS THE MAIN BUILDING BLOCK OF MANY SKATING TRICKS. LEARNING HOW TO OLLIE IS THE FIRST STEP IN LEARNING HOW TO DO GRINDS AND KICKFLIPS AND TO PULL AIR OFF RAMPS.

FIRST, YOU GET ROLLING WITH YOUR BACK FOOT ON THE TAIL AND YOUR FRONT BETWEEN THE MIDDLE OF THE BOARD AND THE FRONT TRUCKS.

WITH YOUR BACK FOOT, SLAP THE TAIL DOWN HARD ON THE GROUND AND THEN JUMP INTO THE AIR AND FORWARD.

BEND YOUR KNEES AND PUSH YOUR FRONT FOOT TOWARD THE NOSE OF THE BOARD. THIS WILL BRING THE BOARD UP TO YOUR FEET AND LEVEL IT OFF.

USE YOUR FEET TO CONTROL THE BOARD WHEN YOU'RE IN THE AIR.

LAND THE BOARD ON ALL FOUR WHEELS AT THE SAME TIME AND BEND YOUR KNEES TO ABSORB THE IMPACT.

THEN RIDE AWAY IN STYLE!

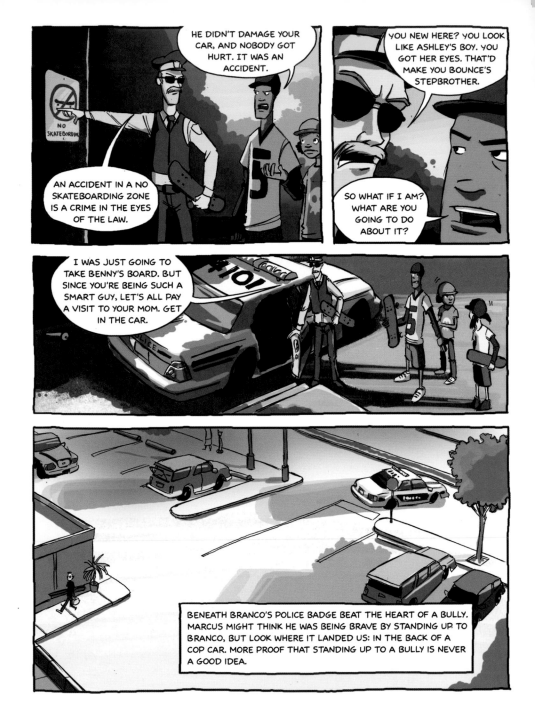

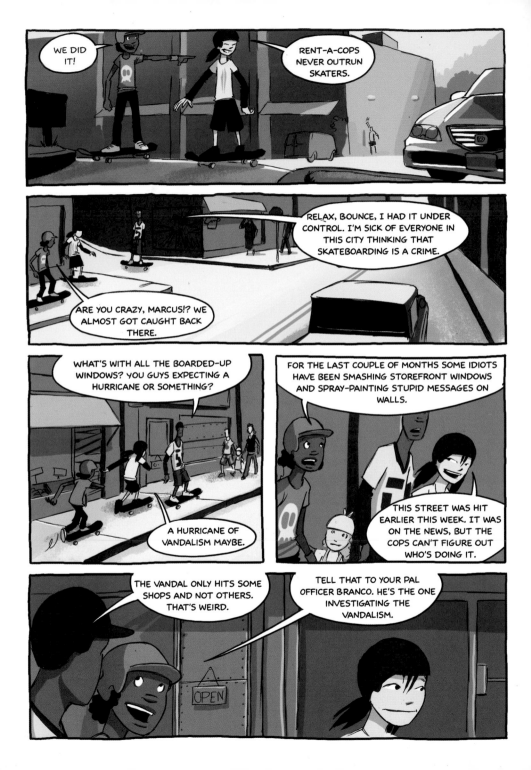

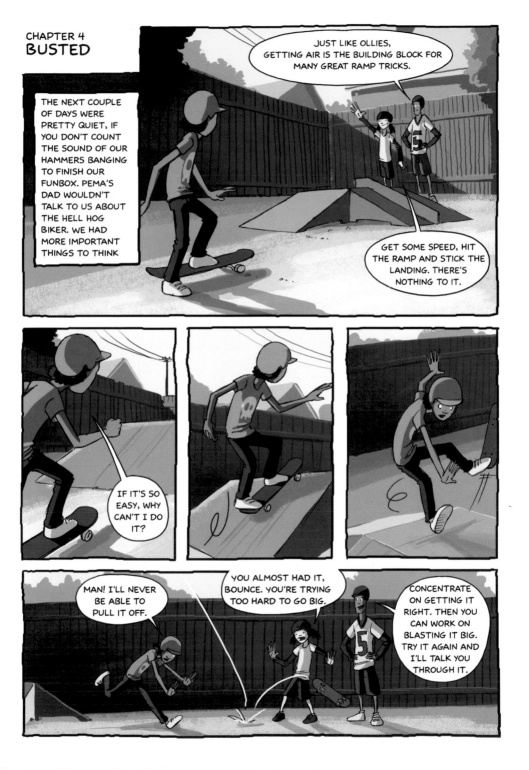

YOUR TURN, PEMA. SHOW BOUNCE HOW TO JUMP WITH STYLE.

ONE STALEFISH COMING UP.

A STALEFISH IS A BASIC AIR THAT LOOKS GREAT. IT'S ALL ABOUT CONTROL AND STYLE. ONCE YOU CAN LAND AN AIR FROM RAMP, YOU'RE READY TO TRY TO PULL A STALEFISH.

FIRST, APPROACH THE RAMP WITH A LOT OF SPEED AND GET READY TO PULL THE BIGGEST AIR YOU CAN.

ONCE YOU LAUNCH OFF THE RAMP, REACH WITH YOUR TRAILING HAND AND GRAB THE BOARD BEHIND AND BETWEEN YOUR LEGS.

NOW YOU'RE READY TO GO FOR STYLE POINTS. BRING YOUR KNEES FLAT AGAINST YOUR DECK AND HOLD IT AS YOU FLY THROUGH THE SKY.

AS YOU START TO LAND, LET GO OF THE BOARD, STRAIGHTEN YOUR LEGS AND GET READY FOR IMPACT.

BEND YOUR KNEES WHEN YOU LAND, KEEP ROLLING AND KEEP LOOKING GOOD!

NOW THAT'S A SERIOUS STALEFISH!

MARCUS WASTED NO TIME ASKING NIMA OUT. AFTER DINNER, HE WAS IN THE BATHROOM POSING AND PREENING IN FRONT OF THE MIRROR NEARLY AN HOUR. THEN HE WAS OUT THE DOOR WITHOUT A WORD.

PEMA WAS MORE ON THE BALL THAN I WAS. SHE GOT THEIR DATE DETAILS AND INSISTED WE FOLLOW THEM.

OKAY, I'VE SEEN ENOUGH. LET'S GO.

NO WAY! YOUR BROTHER DATING MY SISTER IS JUST TOO WEIRD TO MISS. KEEP QUIET OR THEY'LL SPOT US.

WE'RE NOT OLD ENOUGH TO SEE THEIR MOVIE. GUESS WE'LL HAVE TO WAIT OUTSIDE.

THERE'S CRUNCH! I'M NOT HANGING OUT HERE WITH HIM AROUND. LET'S SEE SOMETHING. ANYTHING! I DON'T CARE.

OKAY, BUT YOU'RE BUYING ME A JUMBO POPCORN!

# CHAPTER 6
# RAMP RATS BITE BACK

IT'S NEVER GOOD TO FIND OUT THAT YOUR DAD HAS BEEN PRO-TECTING CRIMINALS. NOT THAT HE HAD MUCH CHOICE. FOR THE PAST YEAR, THE HELL HOG BIKERS HAD BEEN DEMAND-ING PROTECTION MONEY FROM ALL THE BUSINESSES IN TOWN.

AS LONG AS WE PAID, WE WERE PROTECTED.

AND IF YOU DIDN'T PAY OR TALKED TO THE COPS, THEY'D COME AND SMASH YOUR WINDOWS.

THAT'S WHY THE BIKER WAS HARASSING MY DAD!

THE HELL HOGS ARE A BUNCH OF BULLIES, LIKE CRUNCH AND HIS GOONS.

WHY DIDN'T YOU STAND UP TO THE BIKERS, LIKE YOU'RE ALWAYS TELLING ME TO DO WITH CRUNCH?

I GUESS IT'S EASIER TO TALK ABOUT STANDING UP THAN IT IS TO DO THE ACTUAL STANDING.

BUT NOW THAT MARCUS IS GETTING THE BLAME, THE BIKERS MUST BE STOPPED. I'M NOT PAYING THEM ANOTHER DOLLAR.

IF YOU DON'T PAY, THEY'LL COME BACK, WON'T THEY?

YUP. AND I'LL BE WAITING FOR THEM.

GOOD. BECAUSE I HAVE A PLAN TO CATCH THESE BIKERS.

DAD WASN'T CRAZY ABOUT MY IDEA, BUT HE DIDN'T HAVE ANYTHING BETTER. WHEN THE SUN WENT DOWN, WE GOT STARTED.

ARE YOU IN POSITION? GOOD. STAY THERE. ASHLEY WOULD SMASH MY WINDOWS IF SHE KNEW YOU KIDS WERE HERE TONIGHT.

GOOD THING SHE'S GOT A LATE HOUSE-VIEWING TONIGHT. AND DON'T WORRY, WE'LL STAY OUT OF SIGHT.

HANKS PICK UP

0%

WE'VE GOT A GREAT VIEW FROM HERE. MARCUS AND NIMA, ARE YOU IN POSITION?

ON MY WAY THERE NOW.

I CALLED THE POLICE STATION FROM THE HOUSE PHONE. THE CHIEF SAID THAT OFFICER BRANCO IS ON HIS WAY.

GET READY. HERE COME THE HELL HOGS.

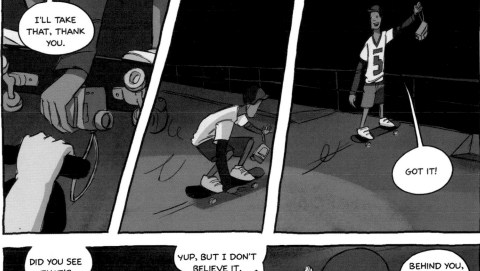

CRASH!

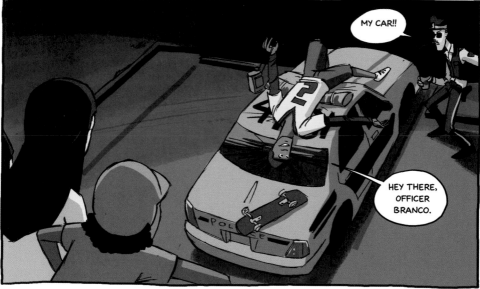

WHETHER YOU'RE RIDING BOWLS, MINI-RAMPS OR HALF-PIPES, KNOWING HOW TO PUMP ON THE TRANSITION IS KEY TO GETTING TO THE COPING AND PULLING TRICKS.

FIRST, GET SOME SPEED AND RIDE TOWARD THE TRANSITION.

WHEN YOU REACH AS FAR AS YOU CAN GO UP THE TRANSITION, STAND UP STRAIGHT AND GET READY TO ROLL BACK DOWN.

AS YOU ROLL DOWN, BEND YOUR KNEES AND PUT YOUR WEIGHT FORWARD. THIS WILL PUSH YOU DOWN THE TRANSITION.

ROLL THROUGH THE FLAT BOTTOM AND INTO THE OPPOSITE TRANSITION. WHEN YOU GET AS HIGH AS YOU CAN GO, STAND UP AGAIN AND GET READY TO ROLL BACK.

I WENT HIGHER THIS TIME!

AS YOU ROLL DOWN THE TRANSITION, BEND YOUR KNEES AND LEAN FORWARD AGAIN. TIME IT RIGHT AND YOU'LL GET MORE SPEED AND GO HIGHER ON THE RAMP EACH TIME.

COOL, I'LL HIT THE LIP THIS TIME FOR SURE.

MADE IT!

*Look for the exciting new installment in the*
*Graphic Guides Adventure series:*

# A GRAPHIC GUIDE ADVENTURE

## ACTION, ADVENTURE AND SOME SPOT-ON SOCCER INSTRUCTION.

Nadia is playing for her local soccer team, and they have made it all the way to the national tournament—against some very determined opposition. Unfortunately, Nadia's challenges don't just come from her opponents but from her teammates as well. After their coach is injured in a suspicious accident and the threats against the team mount, it is up to Nadia and her younger brother Devin to pull the team together and take a run at the championship. Another Wild Ride!

### COMING SPRING 2009!

WRITTEN BY
**LIAM O'DONNELL**

ILLUSTRATED BY
**MIKE DEAS**

FROM CHAPTER BOOKS TO COMIC STRIPS, **LIAM O'DONNELL** WRITES FICTION AND NON-FICTION FOR YOUNG READERS. HE IS THE AUTHOR OF THE AWARD-WINNING SERIES "MAX FINDER MYSTERY." LIAM LIVES IN TORONTO, ONTARIO.

**MIKE DEAS** IS A TALENTED ILLUSTRATOR IN A NUMBER OF DIFFERENT GENRES. HE GRADUATED FROM CAPILANO COLLEGE'S COMMERCIAL ANIMATION PROGRAM AND HAS WORKED AS A GAME DEVELOPER. MIKE LIVES IN VICTORIA, BRITISH COLUMBIA.